Where Will You Go?

Where Will You Go?

Kelle Marie Stavron

&

Matthew William Stavron

July 20, 1983 – September 16, 2007

Shoestring Book Publishing, Maine, USA

Where Will You Go?

Written by Kelle Marie Stavron &
Matthew William Stavron

Paperback

ISBN: 978-1-943974-41-2

Published by;
Shoestring Book Publishing.
Maine, USA

Printed in the United States of America.

Layout and design by Shoestring Book Publishing

For information address;
495 Penobscot Avenue Millinocket Maine 04462
shoestringpublishing4u@gmail.com
www.shoestringbookpublishing.com

Contents

Introduction

This book is a dedication in memory of Matthew William Stavron, our oldest son, brother, grandson, fiancé, uncle, nephew, cousin and friend. Matthew was born July 20, 1983 and passed away on September 16, 2007 from an opiate prescription drug overdose at the young age of twenty-four years old.

These poems were all written by Matthew while sitting in the Orange County jail just one year prior to his passing. Where Will You Go was the first poem he had ever written and we were all very impressed. Who would have thought that these beautiful poetic expressions would become prophetic in reality and beyond the grave? We certainly did not.

Matt was passionate about racing motorcycles along with his brother Bryce and it became our family's sport. Matt's first racing injury took place at the young age of thirteen and this was his first experience with opiate pain medication. Just like so many people in our world today Matthew became a drug addict which also progressed through the years. Matt hated his addiction to drugs just like most addicts do. He felt tormented within his mind and found his faith and belief as his only saving grace. Matthew also achieved many small periods of sobriety during his drug addiction roller coaster ride. The ride he took his family and loves ones on included, many prayers, racing, periods of sobriety, rehab, active drug addiction, injuries, training, church, meetings, jail and other fun times to.

With today's society, drug overdoses and the premature death of our youth have brought so much devastation. It's not only the drug addict that suffers but also their families and friends.

The beautiful part of Matthew was his love for others, his charming personality and his compassionate heart. Just a couple of years before he died he had the idea to start a ministry called "Beyond the Grave", which would help others with pain and opiate addiction. His intention was to start in the motocross industry and expand it to all the people he loves, as well as others that also struggled with addiction. These poems that Matthew wrote are his loving prayers for all of you beyond the grave into God's loving grace just for you.

Our hope and prayer is that you are blessed to embrace your faith and belief. They can assist you throughout your life and with knowing your eternal destiny; a destiny where love, grace and forgiveness may keep us all humble before our Creator and God.

Blessings with all my love, from Matthew's mama always,

Kelle Marie Stavron

We Love you Matthew

Throughout Eternity

and Unto Heavens Skies

The Poetry of

Matthew William Stavron

Thank God I'm Done

While I wait in this cell for my time to go by
I pray to the Lord that he stays by my side
I'm reading his word every morning and night
Through it, he tells me my future looks bright
Every day I grow stronger,
deeper within my heart
It's no longer burning with sin
He has cleansed my soul he's lightened the load
I'm finally happy Satan no longer has a hold
I'm finally free from the bondage of sin
I no longer care for the drugs and old friends
So as I wait, in this cell for my time to go by
I say goodbye to my pride and my lies
It's finally over; I can't wait to come home
The battles been won
Thank God I'm done!!

Notes:

Written 2006. My son wanted me to share this poem for those who still suffer, you don't have to anymore!
One day at a time!!

Thanks Mom

Oh my precious mother
how good you are to me,
your love seems unconditional
and comes without a fee.

Even though right now you're far from me,
just know you're in my heart,
this time will soon go by
and we'll no longer be apart.

We've been through many trials together
you've always stayed by my side,
praying for me, loving on me
and saying it's gonna be alright.

I just wanted to thank you for being there,
and you said you liked my poems.
I love you very much mom
and it won't bc long bcforc I'm home!

Written 2006

Dear Grandma,

No matter what I do you are always there,
saying that you love me and telling me you care.
You make me feel better when my life gets rough,
I love you very much, I could never thank you enough.

Right now I'm in my cell, locked up in county jail,
You still make sure we talk on the phone,
or through the mail.
I miss you every day while I sit in this place,
I can't wait to come home, so I can see your face.

Just know you're in my heart,
which is where you'll always be,
Because you're the best Grandma ever,
is what you are to me.
I love you and miss you Grandma,

Love your grandson,
Matthew William Stavron
October 29, 2006

Note:
This is the fourth and last poem that Matthew had written. He had written a total of four poems in the year before he passed away.

Where Will You Go?

If you were to die tomorrow where would you go?
Heaven sounds nice but do you truly know,
That when you leave this wretched place,
that is where you'll be?
Do you have doubts about your so called beliefs?

This answer is in a book so many people ignore,
the book's everywhere, just look in a hotel drawer.
There are many religions that lie and mislead,
these created by man and the evil he seeks.

The deception and greed, the flesh that we feed,
will all come to an end, then where will you be?
You'll be in one of two places, there's heaven or hell,
when the end is no man can tell.

The final day of judgment you should truly fear,
the sentence is eternity, not a county year!
You'll have no attorney to help you plead your case,
but this judge is different, He's full of love and grace!

He sent His only Son to die for our sins,
we tortured and killed Him like He was no friend.
This man's name is Jesus and he's coming again,
He'll take us who believe in Him to the pearly gates,
the entrance where our Creator awaits!

Here, there's no pain, no evil, no sin.
just eternal happiness with our Father and friends.
The answer is simple, now can you see?
If you'd just read that book then you'd believe!

You'll learn that Jesus is The Way,
you just have to have faith;
He died for our sins, we live under his grace.
This book is called the Bible, you can have one for free,
just go to a church, they won't charge a fee!

Note:

Matthew wrote this poem in pencil in 2006, just one year prior to his passing. Matt told his family he just wanted to share the good news and there is always hope with God and that God is everywhere.

**"When the solution is simple,
God is answering."**
-Albert Einstein

Please Review!

All independent authors depend upon reviews left on Amazon.com by readers to help promote their books. Without these reviews, they will hardly get any notice. Please take the time to leave a short review. Simply go to Amazon.com, find the book and go to the book's page. Under the author's name will be a list of reviews and stars. Click here and there will be a big button saying "Create your own review". Please click here and review.

It only takes a minute!

Made in the USA
Las Vegas, NV
21 June 2026

49442381R00017